P9-DDC-124

REPORT CARD

Name: Knope, Leslie Barbara

Instructor: Albright

Parent Signature:

_____

PAWNEE ELEMENTARY

To my glorious rainbow-infused space-unicorn lady friends: Growing up, I wished for a sister, but I had no idea I would end up with so many. You are each a gift in my life and make every day feel like Galentine's Day, even when we are apart. I love you all. —M. D.

For Audrey, Jen, Jenny, Mary, Michelle, Russell, and Sharona, who always have my vote. —R. P.

© 2021 Universal Television LLC. All Rights Reserved. • Illustrations by Melanie Demmer. • Cover design by Sasha Illingworth. Cover illustration by Melanie Demmer. • Hachette Book Group supports the right to free expression and the value of copyright. The purpose of copyright is to encourage writers and artists to produce the creative works that enrich our culture. • The scanning, uploading, and distribution of this book without permission is a theft of the author's intellectual property. If you would like permission to use material from the book (other than for review purposes), please contact permissions@hbgusa.com. Thank you for your support of the author's rights. • Little, Brown and Company • Hachette Book Group • 1290 Avenue of the Americas, New York, NY 10104 • Visit us at LBYR.com •
First Edition: June 2021 • Little, Brown and Company is a division of Hachette Book Group, Inc. • The Little, Brown name and logo are trademarks of Hachette Book Group, Inc. • The publisher is not responsible for websites (or their content) that are not owned by the publisher. • Library of Congress cataloging-in-publication data is available. • ISBNs: 978-0-316-42865-1 (hardcover), 978-0-316-29902-2 (B&N special edition), 978-0-316-42866-8 (ebook), 978-0-316-42867-5 (ebook), 978-0-316-42869-9 (ebook) • Printed in CHINA • APS •

10 9 8 7 6 5 4 3 2 1

Parks and Recreation
Leslie for Class President!

PAWNEE PRIDE!

Can you find all these things as you read the story?

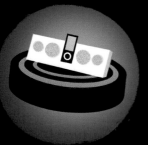

Raccoons

Marshmallow Ron Swanson

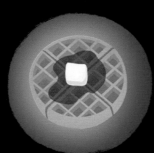

JJ's Diner Waffle

Mark Brendanawicz

DJ Roomba

Li'l Sebastian

Duke Silver

Pawnee Goddesses

Tammy 2

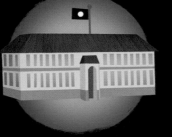

Eagleton

Orin

Mouse Rat

Parks and Recreation

Leslie for Class President!

WRITTEN BY **ROBB PEARLMAN** ★ ILLUSTRATED BY **MELANIE DEMMER**

Little, Brown and Company

New York Boston

"**A** good leader is eager, honest, and responsible. Just like me! I'm Leslie Knope, and I'm running for class president at Pawnee Elementary! When elected, I'll help make this school a better place. We all have the right to life, liberty, and the pursuit of happiness. And waffles!"

VOTE KNOPE

"There are no waffles here, Leslie! So I'm not very happy!" yells Andy. "And I fell into this pit! Could you fix it?"

"You bet I can!" I declare. "In fact, I *promise* to fill this hole. And when it's done, we'll have a party!"

"Awesome! You've got my vote," says Andy. "I'll vote for you lots of times!"

"Everybody gets only one vote," explains Ben. "But every vote counts!"

"Thanks, Ben! And, Ann! You beautiful tropical fish! Thanks for helping me! Please write down 'fill in the pit!'" I say.

"All right, let's go convince our classmates to vote for me," I say. "Did you know that grown-ups call this *lobbying*?"

"Is that why we're in the lobby?" asks Ann.

"That's exactly right, you poetic and noble land-mermaid!" I say.

Ann loves when I find new ways to say how cool she is. Just then, I see some potential voters.

"Donna! Tom!" I shout. "I'd like to tell you why
I would make a great class president."

"Sorry, we don't have time to talk," Donna says.
"It's October thirteenth!"

"Oh right. Happy Treat Yo Self Day!" I squeal.

"What's Treat Yo Self Day?" asks Ben.

Donna gasps. Tom falls down.

PAWNEE GODDESSES

SIGN UP:

KNOPE

Ben is new, so he doesn't know about our holidays. February thirteenth is Galentine's Day. August thirteenth is Haircut Day. And August fourteenth is Second Haircut Day!

BOBBY
TEAM PAWNEE
But you'd think he'd at least know about Treat Yo Self Day. It's when you buy yourself gifts. All. Day. Long.

"Hey, Leslie," Donna says, "if you become president, can you get school canceled on all Treat Yo Self Days?"
"Uh...of course I can!" I promise.

Donna says, "In that case, you've got our votes!"
"Ann, you rainbow-infused space unicorn, please jot that down," I ask.

Vote Leslie B. Knope for class President
Treat Yo Self Day sounds like the best day ever! I'm going to celebrate by eating only calzones. And there's nothing my mom can do to stop me.

Then we bump into Chris.

"Ben Wyatt! Ann Perkins!" says Chris. "Leslie Knope! You're running for class president?! That's fantastic! Me? I'm just running to the cafeteria!"

"Yes, and when I'm president," I say, "we'll have Waffle Wednesday!"

"Can you promise a gluten-free vegan option?" Chris asks.

"Sure," I say slowly. "I promise!"

"That's *lit*erally the best news I've heard all week! You've got my vote," says Chris.

"Ann, you opalescent tree shark, I guess you should write down that promise, too," I say.

I spend the rest of the day handing out binders and making even more promises.

I promise Jerry a puppy.

I promise
Garth we'll
start a Castles &
Creatures club.

And I promise
Jean-Ralphio hip-hop
dance classes in gym.

I'm not sure how I'm going to keep all my promises, but it's time to hand in my forms so I can get on the ballot.
Leslie has to give her forms to Ron, who will give them to our teacher, Miss Beavers, who will then officially put Leslie on the ballot. I wonder why she can't just give the forms right to Miss Beavers.
Why?! It's called *BUREAUCRACY*!
KNOPE

Bureaucracy is *EXCITING*! It means you get to do lots of extra, cool work. I bet feminists like Susan B. Anthony and Ida B. Wells would agree. Actually, my middle name is Barbara, so maybe I am destined to support bureaucracy, which also starts with a *B*!
KNOPE
Vote Leslie B. Knope!

On my way to give Ron my forms, I see
another potential voter.

"April!" I say. "Can I count on your vote?"

April rolls her eyes. "Ugh, only if you promise
to leave me alone."

SHOP ROOM

RON'S office

"You bet! So you'll vote for me?" I ask.

"Okay, yeah, sure, whatever. I don't care," she says.

I look down at my very long list of promises. I guess I'll write down that one myself....

I've made so many promises
to so many people today. What
if I can't make them all happen?
What if I let my classmates down?

What if...I shouldn't be class president?

I shuffle through the door to see Ron.
"Maybe I shouldn't give my forms to you," I tell Ron.
"I don't think I can be president."
"Why not?" Ron asks as he puts down his hammer.
"Because I can't keep all the promises I made." I sigh.

"Do you know why I like woodworking?" Ron asks me. "The wood knows exactly what it's supposed to be, and it doesn't need to be more than that. See this birdhouse? It isn't trying to be a harp. Just being a sanctuary for the northern cardinal is enough."

"Leslie," Ron asks, "what are the qualities of a good leader?"

"They should be eager, honest, and responsible," I mumble.

"Well, you were eager enough to make all those promises. You're honest enough to admit that you might not be able to keep all of them. And I know you're responsible enough to try your best. That sounds like a leader to me. Leslie, you are the birdhouse," he says.

"So, you think I'd make a good president?" I ask.

"It doesn't matter what I think. What do you think?"

"*I* am enough!" I say. "I *can* do this!"

"Great," Ron says as he picks up his hammer.

"Now get out of my workshop."

I can do what I want.

-Ron

The next day, Bobby and I give speeches in front of our classmates. He only talks about giving out free candy and tours of the Sweetums factory. I have lots more to say.

"Fellow students, I can't promise you a never-ending supply of candy. I can't even promise that I'll be able to make all my promises happen right away...or ever. Sorry, Jerry.

"But I *can* promise that I'll do *my* best to make Pawnee Elementary the best *it* can be! Please vote Leslie B. Knope!"

"I am honored to be your president, and I am going to work hard for you! My first presidential act will be to fill this pit!" I declare. The crowd cheers.

As my friends enjoy my victory party, Ben says, "I knew you could do it! The pit will be filled in no time. But I've gotta ask—are you ready for what's next?"

Sweetums

CAUTION KEEP OUT CAUTION KEEP OUT CAUTION KEEP OUT CAUTION KEEP O

KEEP OUT CAUTION KEEP OUT CAUTION KE

I look around at all my friends and
think about the future and say, "I am!"

JJ's
Diner

Syrup

WORLD-FAMOUS
...ES